THE DEEP DARK WOODS

Turn the page to start the story.

THE DEEP DARK WOODS

Written by Conrad Mason

Illustrated by Ben Mantle

How this book works

The story of **The Deep Dark Woods** has been written for you to read with your child. You take turns to read.

You read these words.

"Beware, beware the deep dark woods."

Do not go far from the pool. Be good!

Your child reads these words.

You don't have to finish the story in one session. If your child is getting tired, put a marker in the page and come back to it later.

You can find out more about helping your child with this book, and with reading in general, on pages 30-31.

5

"Join me, Dan,
it will be good fun."

It is cold in the woods,
full of shadows and mist.

"This is no fun.
Can we go now, Jack?"

"But Dan, I am not sure how to get back!"

Then a crash and a cry
gives the pair a fright.

Woooooooooo!

"Is that a wail,
a howl or a yell?"

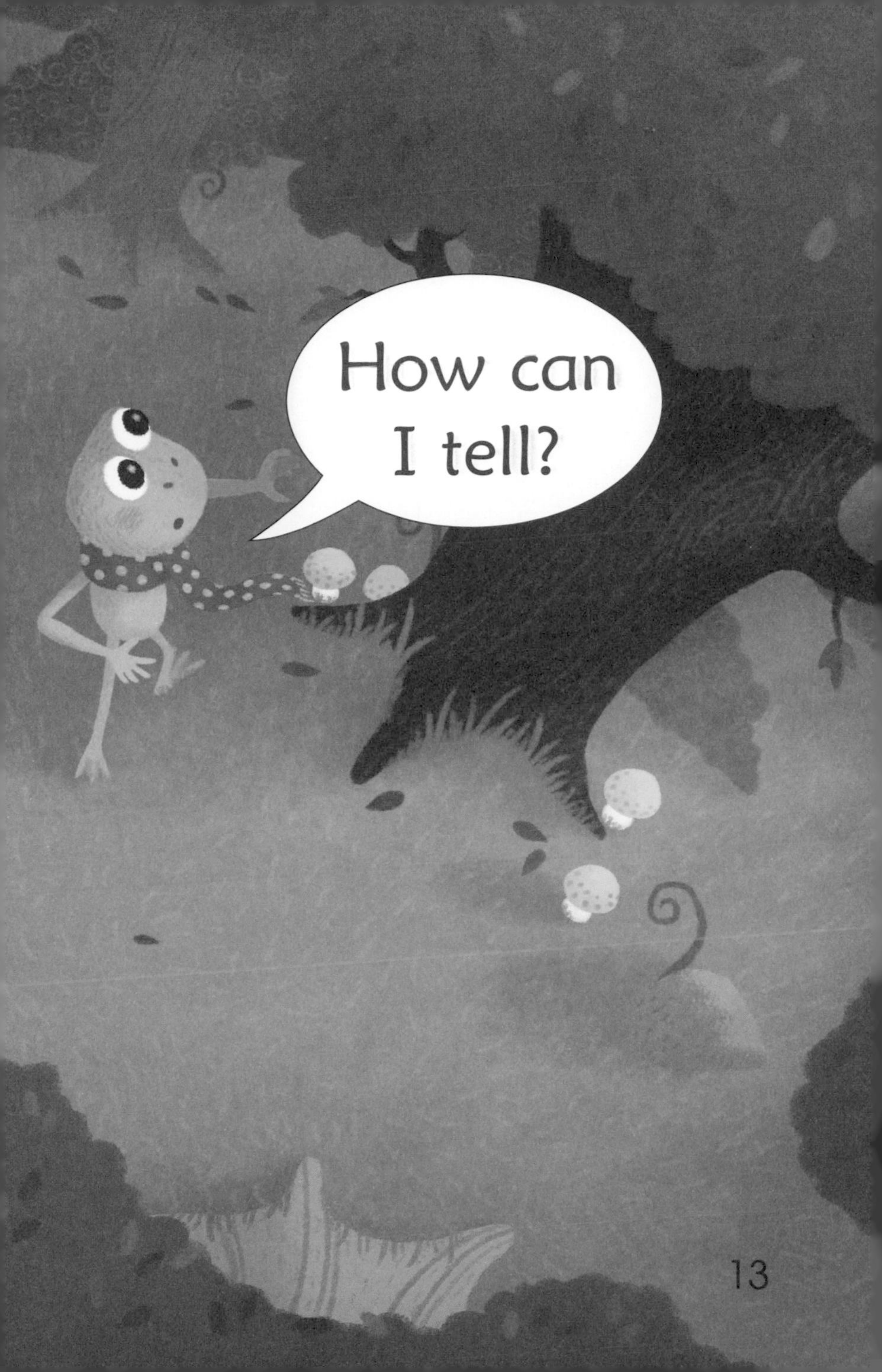
How can I tell?

"It's a ghost! A monster!
A horrible brute!"

Toooo-woooo!

No, now I can hear, I am sure it's a hoot.

"Look! It's an owl,
    trapped under a tree."

"Do you need to get home?
Let me take you there."

Jack and Dan and the
owl zoom up in the air.

The owl sets them down,
and they wave goodbye.

23

Puzzle 1

Are these sentences true? Look at the pictures and say what really happened.

1.

Jack will be good, he will not go far.

2.

It is such fun for Dan in the dark.

3.

Jack and Dan can
hear a fox bark.

4.

Jack and Dan cannot
set the owl free.

5.

The owl is sure to
hurt Jack and Dan.

Puzzle 2

Choose the right word to complete each phrase.

1.

Do not go......

tar	car	far

2.

......can I tell?

Cow	How	Now

3.

Now tug......, Dan.

| card | hard | lard |

4.

Up in the ......

| air | hair | fair |

Puzzle 3

Match the speech bubbles to the pictures.

Answers to puzzles

Puzzle 1
(Your child doesn't have to use these exact words.)

1. No, Jack is going to the woods.

2. No, Dan wants to go home.

3. No, they can hear an owl hoot.

4. No, they do set it free.

5. No, the owl takes them safely home.

Puzzle 2

1. Do not go <u>far</u>.

2. <u>How</u> can I tell?

3. Now tug <u>hard</u>, Dan.

4. Up in the <u>air</u>.

Puzzle 3

1. C Join me, Dan.

2. A Will it hurt us?

3. B I will not go back.

Guidance notes

Usborne Very First Reading is a series of books, specially developed for children who are learning to read. In the early books in the series, you and your child take turns to read, and your child steadily builds the knowledge and confidence to read alone.

The words for your child to read in **The Deep Dark Woods** introduce these letter-combinations:

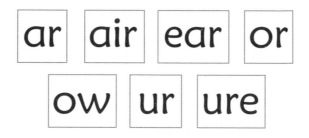

It's well worth giving your child plenty of practice reading these. Later books in the series introduce longer words and new spelling patterns, while reinforcing the ones your child already knows.

You'll find lots more information about the structure of the series, advice on helping your child with reading, extra practice activities and games on the Very First Reading website,* **www.usborne.com/veryfirstreading**

*US readers go to **www.veryfirstreading.com**

Some questions and answers

- **Why do I need to read with my child?**
  Sharing stories and taking turns makes reading an enjoyable and fun activity for children. It also helps them to develop confidence and reading stamina, and to take part in an exciting story using very few words.

- **When is a good time to read?**
  Choose a time when you are both relaxed, but not too tired, and there are no distractions. Only read for as long as your child wants to – you can always try again another day.

- **What if my child gets stuck?**
  Don't simply read the problem word yourself, but prompt your child and try to find the right answer together. Similarly, if your child makes a mistake, go back and look at the word together. Don't forget to give plenty of praise and encouragement.

- **We've finished, now what do we do?**
  It's a good idea to read the story several times to give your child more practice and confidence. Then you can try reading **Stop that Cow!** at the same level or, when your child is ready, go on to Book 8 in the series.

Edited by Jenny Tyler, Mairi Mackinnon
and Lesley Sims
Designed by Caroline Spatz

First published in 2011 by Usborne Publishing Ltd., Usborne House,
83-85 Saffron Hill, London EC1N 8RT, England. www.usborne.com
Copyright © 2011 Usborne Publishing Ltd.